CW01468035

RUOK?

RUOK?

—————

A HORROR STORY IN TEXTS

ANDY FUTURO

JUNE DAY PRESS

Copyright © 2024 by Andy Futuro

All rights reserved.

No part of this book may be reproduced in any form or by any electronic or mechanical means, including information storage and retrieval systems, without written permission from the author, except for the use of brief quotations in a book review.

ISBN: 9798340147202

To Rori. I'm sorry.

Hey Rori...

It's James

I got a new number

I know it's been a little while

I heard what happened...

I'm really sorry

MISSED CALL

[Pajamacat.png]

Here's a picture of a cat in pajamas

Hope it cheers you up

MISSED CALL

Hey I know you're going through a lot right now

Could you please just respond so I know you're okay?

No

I'm not okay

Nothing is ok

Yeah...

I'm sure it will feel that way for a while

How's your mom taking it?

The worst

She acts like nothing happened

All business

I think she's trying to keep it together for me

But I can hear her crying in the bathroom

Yeah...

How's Bean?

Angry

He punched a hole in the wall yesterday when mom told him to stop playing Fortnite and do his homework

Mom started screaming

And he just ran out the door

Then mom was crying and telling me we had to go look for him. And I was like no mom, we're not going to take flashlights and crawl around in the dark looking for him. He just needs space

You're sucking up all the oxygen again

Seriously, I'm the only adult left in the house

Like

This is why dad "went off to heaven." He got wrapped around a truck grill because he was driving around at 2am looking for some peace

Well he found it

Dad would have liked that joke

Don't tell my mom

Aaaaaaaaauuuuurrrrrrgggggghhhhh

I'm so angry I could rip my skin off

Mom...ugh

It's horrible I'm even thinking it. But now I'm trapped in the house with her and Bean and the grief and none of us can handle it

I wish it was her

I CAN'T BREATHE

She's supposed to be the parent, but it's like I'm taking care of her

It's okay mom, we're okay, all fine

I feel like I'm 16 going on 60

Sorry that was a lot

Didn't mean to dump on you like that

It's okay

Hugs

I'm so, so sorry

That sounds really hard

Do whatever you need

I'm here for you

Thanks :)

I want to say I wish you were here but I don't. I mean I do. I really, really wish you were here. But I'm glad you got out of this crappy little town

This whole place smells like death

As soon as I turn 18 I'm gone. I'm already saving all my babysitting money for a car. I'll take dad's ashes and drive straight across the country to California

Start a new life. Get a job. I'll make my own money and never have to rely on anyone for anything again

I'll take Bean with me if he wants to go

But he'll probably be in jail by then

That's dark

Dad said only people who see the darkness in life can also see the light

But I guess he couldn't even see the headlights coming right at him

...

Are you seeing anyone?

A therapist?

Lol

I'm not saying there's anything wrong with you. I see a therapist. It can really help work through things

I'm not anti-therapy

But even when dad was working construction we didn't have enough money to fix Bean's cavities.

We had to take the bus 3 hours down to a free clinic in the parking lot of a mall

And after dad hurt his back...

And took the security guard job

Let's just say they weren't paying him millions to sit in a little booth and stare at an abandoned building all night

Yeah...

What if...I could start a fundraiser? Raise money for you...

I'm sure people would pitch in

...

I'm going to pretend you didn't just say that so we can stay friends.

Sorry...

I was just trying to help

Let me know if there's anything I can do

I know...

This is helping...

Just you being here

Listening

You're the only one who listens

SEPTEMBER 10

Hey

Bean found something

He was going through dad's stuff and he found a dvd dad had burned

A DVD

Isn't that weird?

Why not use his phone?

And on it was a recording of him saying goodbye

Mom and Bean were bawling

And then mom called me cold and unloving for not reacting

But I was just sitting there thinking, like, this is so weird

Like. Why would he make this?

He died in a car crash

It's not like he had terminal cancer or something

It was dated a month ago. So he went out and bought a DVD burner and video camera to record this for us

Like, he put a lot of thought into it

He couldn't know he was going to die

Right???

Yeah, that's odd

But parents are weird. They do weird things all the time

Like my mom wanted us to go to Legoland the other day and I was like, mom, we were too old for Legoland three years ago

Hmmm

Maybe

And now mom's getting on my case for being heartless and not spending enough time with her

She called me selfish again

Maybe she's right though

I haven't even asked about you

How are things? How's Colorado

?

It's okay. The school is a lot bigger. Literally thousands of kids. There are a lot of cliques, but they're so big they're like your warband

Lol

They make fun of me for my accent. I thought in Colorado maybe they wouldn't notice but

They notice alright

Jefferson county PA

We're the hickest of hicks

Can you call people hicks these days?

You can if you are one

Try to lose the accent if you can. It will take you father in life

Farther

Freudian slip

Ha

What warband are you going to join?

I think it'll be the marching band geeks

They seem to be pretty cool and friendly

Solid choice

Put your clarinet skills to use

Who else is in the running?

There's the D&D club

Not what you'd expect

A surprising number of jocks

And they have 2 dungeon masters, both of them are theatre kids so they're really dramatic and they even do dialogues between the characters together

Wow

Yeah but

I don't know if I want that to be my warband

Why not?

At least they know how to use weapons

And cast spells :)

[Catcastingspell.jpeg]

Lol

But really

Why not?

You love D&D

I do

But is it really the thing I want most known about me?

I'm hoping this is a chance to start fresh

You know how bad things were at Jefferson High

Yeah

I just don't want to give anyone a reason to bully me

[Sadface.jpeg]

Can't you join two clubs?

I'll be lucky to get accepted to one

They're so cliquey

It's like, you can join any club

But if you aren't

In

Then you're not in

They'll be really mean to you

Or kind of ignore you

Or exclude you

When I first got here I joined this pretentious drawing club

Everyone was kind of snooty to me

I couldn't figure out why

They always judged my drawings really hard

Like mean

And not constructive

And they always gave me the worst supplies

And would "forget" to tell me things

Like they all went on this field trip

To an architecture museum

Somehow they "forgot" to tell me

They kept it a secret for days

Went to a lot of work to exclude me

I was the only member of the club who didn't go

They were all out having fun and I was at school

Even kids not in the club knew about the field trip

And they were like

"Why are you here?"

Yeah

Why am I here?

I quit

Uuurrgghhh

That sucks

It was humiliating

I'm sorry

That's why you have to pick the right group

Smaller clubs are harder to get into

But the people are "cooler"

You're cool

I don't need to be cool

I'm fine being the chubby

Clarinet playing

Level 19 paladin

Just you saying that is cool

Stop

Stop being cool

But the thing is

The bigger groups are pretty much the clubs and extracurriculars that have to let anybody in

The boardgame club

Or dodgeball club

Trust me

You don't want to be in dodgeball club

They're basically orcs

Lol

Why not start your own warband?

Hmmm

Most warlords don't ride into battle with no one following them

I'd follow you :)

Thanks

:)

Ugh

Gotta go

Bean is having a meltdown and mom is crying again

Gotta go put out fires

SEPTEMBER 12

You are not going to believe what I found

Oh boy

I've been watching the tape dad left on repeat

Why are you doing that to yourself?

Because I found a code

No

Yes

This is a bad thought

Please let it go

No I'm sure

Morse code. He blinks in morse code

Kind of obvious, dad

But the first clue is always easy

I typed it out

It reads "attic ray"

Or he said nothing

Because it means nothing

No

I watched the tape a thousand times

It's right at the end when he starts to tear up

He blinks it out in morse code

Or he was literally blinking the tears from his eyes

No he cried to hide it

And put it at the end

So I could rewind it quickly

And decode it

I'm going up to the attic

To look for a man named Ray?

Brb

Don't do this

Hello?

Well I found it

What?

The next clue

:/

I went into the attic and picked through all the crap looking for ray or possibly "yar"

Since dad liked putting things backward

Maybe it was a pirate thing

Yar

Smh

[headshake.gif]

But it was just an Indiana Jones thing

All afternoon the sunlight shines through the little window in the cupola

It shines right at dad's old dartboard

Or like around it

Sometimes on it

But it's obvious

A ray of light

There's nothing else it could be pointing at

You know if you do this you're not going to find your dad at the end, right?

What??

Is that what you think?

That my dad faked his own death

To get out of debt

Or get away from mom

Or ditch me and Bean?

That's not what I meant

Oh yeah

I'm sure after solving dad's final puzzle game

My prize will be finding him

The last clue will lead me to a diner

He'll be sitting there

Drinking coffee

Alive

I'm sorry

Oh hi Sprout

You found me

Good to see you

I'm sorry

You solved the game

Give your dad

Who's still alive

A hug

:(:(:(

I meant metaphorically

Spiritually

You mean it's all in my head

Grief

It hath made me crazy!

I'm solving imaginary puzzles

To distract myself from the fact

That my dad's dead

[Hug.gif]

That's what you meant

I just meant it is not good for you

In any case

No matter what

Like

Imagine this is real

Oh thanks

I see you take me very seriously

Listen

I know when my dad is starting a puzzle game

We must have played dozens

Hundreds

Growing up was really freaking dark

Mom and dad were always fighting

Or at least mom was fighting at dad

And we never had money for anything

Everything we ate came out of a box and all my clothes came from the Salvation Army store

But I thought it was magical

Because dad made it magical with his puzzle games

I wasn't worried about the lights going off

I was busy searching the basement by candlelight for treasure

And even though it was usually just Skittles or a dollar or a little plastic toy at the end

It felt like I'd found gold bars and jewels

Dad loved me so damn much he spent his free time trying to make my life feel like an adventure

Even when I was too old for it it was fun

Just the challenge

To see if I could get inside his head and figure it out

Dad always started the games with an easy clue

A cryptic note arriving in the mail

A new poster on the wall with a puzzle written on the back

A garden gnome appearing on the lawn with a map buried underneath

A suspicious box in the closet wrapped in duct tape

Dad would even blink morse code to me at the dinner table

Telling me where I could find a clue

So don't tell me this is fake

...

I hear you

Do you?

You can see how this is different though

Right?

I'm just not making any assumptions

It's like

If this is one of your dad's puzzle games

It's cursed

He started it in really poor taste

And then

You know

What's it going to do for you?

Playing his game?

Playing *this* game?

It would remind me of the best times I ever had with my dad

Probably in my life

Gosh

You're right

That is so wrong

:|

:(

Ugh

I'm sorry I tried to tell you how to grieve

But I wouldn't do this

Well let's hope you never have to find out if that's true

Oof okay

I'm sorry

Really

It's fine

I'm just *dying* to tell you

I found a key

Pressed into the back cork of the dartboard

What a coincidence

You're supposed to say

A key

A key to what?

That's the obvious question

A key

A key to what?

That's the obvious question!

With an obvious answer

He scratched RIP into the metal

And the other side has a splotch of white paint

Or maybe white-out

It has to be where we buried Mrs. White

Please don't tell me you're going to dig up your mom's pet rabbit's grave

It's empty

Mrs. White ran away

Bean and I helped her escape

I left the hatch unlocked

Then Bean told mom he saw Mrs. White get eaten by coyotes

So I guess there was a revenge element to it

We dug a fake grave

It's empty

Dad was in on it

Or at least we told him later

And he didn't tell mom

I hope wherever you are

You're happy

You got out

Mrs. White

And if there's nothing there?

Are you going to just rob another grave?

Ha

I knew you'd be sassy about this

So I already dug up the grave and found this

[Metalbox.jpeg]

What

I'm not sure if you're pranking me

Or not

It's a lock box

Four letter code

Huh

I haven't seen any code anywhere

Maybe it's in the video

I could always smash it open

But that could damage whatever's inside

Any thoughts?

Your birthday

I already tried the birthdays of family members

And major holidays

And the day he died

To see if he knew

Knew...

Something

But that didn't work

If it opened for any of our birthdays

I thought I might find a note

Or something

Or maybe some cash or jewels or something he was hiding from the collections agency

No luck

1234

I tried that too

And twenty other common easy passwords

But ten digits across four slots means

10^4

Possible combinations

That's

10,000

No way to brute force it

Yeah

Maybe if you were a computer

Dang

I need to think about this

I have to find that code

5

SEPTEMBER 14

It was easy

Where did we see numbers before?

RIP

3

I tried codes that were all multiples of 3

3333

3336

But then I realized that would be impossible

So I tried

Atticray

8

Multiples of 8?

No the multiples weren't helpful

Maybe numbers that sum to 8

Click

No

Yeah

Here's how I figured it out

Ray = 3

Attic = 5

There are a couple different ways to get a sum of 8 while first making a sum of 3 and 5

0035

1205

3113

Etc.

But the most intuitive is to use three 1s

Also the 3 in ray could indicate 3 digits as well as a sum of 3

Since you couldn't go the other way

And think 5 digits on a four-digit combo lock

So the code is

1115

Wow

I don't think I would have figured that out in a million years

You didn't grow up doing this

It's easier for me because I know how dad thinks

Not only that but

1115 is a pretty bad code for a lock

You don't have three tumblers in the same position in a row

Which means it's a bad code on purpose

It's not to keep me out

It's to make me go on

It's to show me this is significant

Pay attention

That sounds a little like a reach

It sounds like dad

Just ask me what was in the box!

You're doing this all wrong

Gasp

What was in the box?!

Nothing

It was empty

Are you serious!!!!

After all that

Yeah

Empty

Except for this

[Upload failed]

The picture isn't going through

Urgh this stupid town

Stupid mountains

We live in the third world

It's because we don't have any cell towers

Really?

Yeah

It's what dad would say

He said that's why they built Stillwater lab here originally

No internet

No cell towers

Middle of nowhere

And then once it was built Stillwater blocked any cell towers being put in

I guess the signals interfered with their research

Or they didn't want anyone to be able to call for help

Too real

I know dad never had service when he went to work

Couldn't even watch youtube

I don't even think he had gps

Not even satellite coverage

Okay just tell me please

I need to know

What's in the box

It's a copy of Diablo

What?

It's a CD copy of Diablo

Dad's favorite videogame

I think this could be the end

Really?

Maybe

I have to accept the possibility

It was dad's favorite game

There's no obvious clue

Maybe this is the prize

One last good memory

It's a nice idea

Of course I have to play it to be sure

There could be a clue in there somewhere

6

SEPTEMBER 15

I just had the worst experience of my life

I was in D&D club

And my party was fighting a basilisk

Like a giant magical snake lizard

And then it was my turn

I attacked

The DM rolled for the basilisk

And said that I was turned to stone

No big deal. My party could get a scroll of stone to flesh and turn me back to normal

But they never did

They won the fight and kept playing

And left my character behind as a statue

And every time it was my turn the DM said "You're stone you can't do anything"

It gets so much worse

I started to feel funny when I got home

Like a pain in my gut

Which was me trying to lay an egg

Turns out I was violently constipated

They had slipped Imodium in my Coke

I had to miss a day of school

Because of a medical emergency

That was me drinking prune juice

And crying on the toilet

Hello?

Aren't you going to say anything to that

?

7

SEPTEMBER 17

Sorry sorry sorry

It's been a rough couple of days

That stinks so much I'm sorry

Those people are jerks

Mom took my phone

I went to play diablo and looked for dad's computer but it was gone

I confronted mom

She said someone from Stillwater took it

His cell phone too

Apparently right after he died

They searched the whole house and took a bunch of his stuff

While Bean and I were at school

Said it was "company property"

What the heck?

I called mom stupid

Hello?! Fourth amendment

Don't just give our stuff away to anyone in a uniform

She grounded me and hid my phone

I just got it back

That's so horrible

I'm sorry it happened

Yeah

It was bad

I don't want to go to school

I hate it here

[Catsighing.gif]

I thought it would be different

Okay

I won't assume you're ignoring me

It's the mountains

Or your mom

8

SEPTEMBER 18

Sorry!!!

Mom took my phone again

I'm really sorry

That's horrible

Don't go to school!

Run away!

School is stupid

Just drop out

You can get a job anywhere

Lots of smart people never graduated high school

Like dad

I'm still working on the Diablo puzzle

I'm so angry they took his computer

Where the heck am I going to get a computer that can play CD games?

Ebay?

Yeah

I wish I could run away

I'll go with you

Where will we go?

Mexico

To a beach somewhere

Like the Shawshank Redemption

I never saw that

But sure

The guy escapes prison tunneling through the wall with a spoon

And then goes to live on a beach

We could do it

Really

We're basically adults with what we've been through

I'm more of an adult than mom

At least I don't cry when someone sets a boundary and then spend all day browsing minion memes on Facebook

I don't feel like an adult

Adults don't get turned to stone by their D&D club

Yeah they do

It looks different

But they do

We can make our own decisions

You wouldn't really run away would you?

I'd run away right now

If it weren't for dad's puzzle

Maybe that's why he did it

To keep me here

He probably knew I'd peace out when I lost my only ally

But I'm still working on the premise dad didn't know he was going to die

So that doesn't make sense

Unless

Unless he thought he was in danger

He wasn't

You know that, right?

Your dad was not in danger

I just can't discount the possibility

Then there could be secret government documents on this Diablo disk

Or plans to a nuclear bomb

0%

There is a 0% chance of that

More likely the disk contains company secrets

That's plausible

Try and rule it out in your head

Giant evil corporate military contractor private army CIA front company Stillwater has dark secret they'll do anything to protect

You can't do it

Too possible

Just think of the companies that strip mined the town and dumped all those chemicals in the lake

Now we have double the national cancer rate

And triple the national suicide rate

0.000001%

So you agree it's possible

No

At that probability level

We can also fly

And shoot lasers from our eyes

And gold rains from the sky

Maybe

After we discover the deep dark secret

But really not

Because if it were true they'd be sending out goons to try and find the disk

Or at least ask about it

Or something

But

But but but

[Butt.gif]

But what if that is the clue

Stillwater

The company dad worked for

The company came by to take his phone and computer

And who knows what else

Whatever

Nothing odd about that

Nothing worth thinking about

I didn't even notice it happened

But now I need to play the game

And it leads me to dad's old computer

But now the computer is not there

Why not?

The company took it

Dad's telling me Stillwater is involved

0.000000000001%

Of course I'll find a way to play the game and be sure there's nothing hidden on the disk

I stole mom's credit card

So money's no object

Please tell me that's a joke

Relax

A CD rom drive is like $20

On Amazon

She won't even notice

And I'll buy some lingerie

And a bucket of candy corn

And if mom notices

I'll say it's a scammer buying things with her card

You'd better buy a jetpack too so you can escape when she finds out

I do this all the time

It's fine

Reparations

:|

9

SEPTEMBER 24

Well I beat the game three times

Once as the warrior, dad's favorite

Then as the mage

Then as the rogue

Nothing

No secrets

No coded messages

No reminders of places we used to go together

Just a sore wrist

My cryptologist didn't find anything either

Cryptologist?

My expert in cryptology

Codes and stuff

Cryptography

No cryptology sounds cooler

You don't have a cryptoanything

Sure I do

It's me

With some help from the internet

I scanned the disk for any hidden files

It's clean

How can you know that?

You know what's funny?

I was asking you:

How can you be so sure there's nothing on the disk?

And now you're asking me that same question

Let that sink in

[Eyeroll.gif]

Anyway

I know because dad wasn't a cryptomagist

Also not a word

And he knew I'm not a cryptofragulist

You are committed to this bit

So he wouldn't make a puzzle

That required me to be a

Cryptomaguffin

Cryptomcmuffin

Unless he is specifically sending me to a cryptomasterologist

That he knows

Which seems unlikely

Oh "that's" what's unlikely

Not all of this

I'm just ruling out obvious possibilities

Now that I have done so

The most likely clue is that dad wanted me to notice Stillwater took his computer

Do I have to get it back

Are the files there?

There are no files

I just can't discount that possibility

But breaking into Stillwater isn't my first move

They probably already read that

And sent out a strike team to get you

Probably

Just joking Stillwater

[Wink.gif]

These are jokes NSA

Just two innocent teenagers joking

Yes

Just jokes

You will not believe this

Mom forgot to pay the water bill

Or something

There's something wrong with the plumbing

No water

No flushes

Helllooooo!?

You have to fix the plumbing

You can't just cry about it

You have to do it

You can't behave like this for days

What?

You don't have water?

No

For real

For like two days

That is not okay

Right?

11

SEPTEMBER 30

I am so stupid

Water's back by the way

I called the plumber

Beech tree got its roots in the pipes

It'll have to come down

But all this time I've been playing the game

Diablo

I watched dozens of playthroughs

I listened to the soundtrack

I even checked the forums

To see if dad had a profile

There or something

With more information

But the clue was on the disk the whole time

Literally on it

I can't believe I missed it

A little N scratched in the disk

And then halfway down the circumference is a notch

It's another clue

Are you sure it's an "N"

It could be a "Z"

Or a scratch

Just like the notch

No it's an N

I already know what to do with it

Guess

An N in the side and a notch

Not much to go on

Maybe it's just normal wear and tear on an ancient CD

No

That's not a real guess

I dunno

It's a dial

You turn it

Kind of!

It's a compass!

N is North

And the notch mark is a direction I will have to travel

Big problem with this

You would have to stand in a very specific spot for that to work

I'm on it

That's obviously the next puzzle to solve

Where to stand and how far to go

Okay but

That's assuming the cd is a compass

How do you make a compass out of a cd?

Is that a joke?

No

How?

It's easy

I'll just glue a magnet to the spot dad labeled N

And then put the cd magnet in a bowl of water

Or something where it can move freely

And the magnet will automatically align north

Does that really work?

Only if you believe compasses are guided by the magnetic poles

And not ghosts or wizards

I did this with dad as a science project

That's probably what he was going for

I can't believe I missed it

Must've repressed that memory for some reason

Probably because it was happy

:/ :/ :/

Dang I don't remember where we made it

That would be helpful

Wait

What if you're supposed to put it on something

Like through the center

It could be that...like what?

Okay just brainstorming here...

Paper towel holder

Finger

Pen or pencil

Carrot

Okay I'm out of ideas

It's probably the carrot

That was dad's favorite food

Really?

No, it was Flaming Hot Cheetos

Though carrots were Mrs. White's favorite food

I think a cd hole could fit a Cheeto

But actually I think you're on to something

Really?

Because I don't

Brb

Uh

Hello?

That was it?

I think

What was?

Cheetos?

Food

Kitchen

Dad would always say our kitchen was hot as hell

He'd be cooking in his underwear

It would get so hot

And he'd say

"It's hot as the fires of hell in here"

Hell

Diablo

I never played Diablo

What's the connection?

In Diablo you fight your way down to hell to slay the demon also called Diablo

The kitchen has to be the place

Does it?

Why not the radiator?

Or the fireplace?

Good thoughts

I'll try there if this doesn't work

Ok gotta go

Uh

Bye

Ugh

I heard my parents arguing about why I wasn't making any friends in the new school

Nothing confirms your loserness like having your parents argue about what a loser you are

You're not a loser!

They're losers

I definitely feel like a loser

Everyone at school knows what happened in D&D club

They're whispering and laughing at me

They smell blood

I'm starting to get a reputation as an easy target

Some kid slapped my lunch tray down in the cafeteria

It was humiliating

The other kids are picking on me to take the attention off themselves

I went to English with applesauce all over my pants

I hate this

I don't know what to do

Transfer maybe

Try again

Drop out

That sucks

Maybe you could beat someone up

Like in prison

Kick the snot out of someone

Then they'd leave you alone

That's not funny

I'm serious

At least they'd stop picking on you

Though I guess Bean gets in fights all the time and they still pick on him

I'm not a fighter

I'm definitely not a fight winner

I'm actually worried someone is going to do that to me

Like I'm legit concerned for my safety

And the teachers don't care

They can't touch the kids

And they don't want to get beat up either

In the other high school in town some kid got jumped

They planned it

A bunch of kids were in on it

At lunch like five kids started punching and kicking him

A bunch of other kids were filming it

Nearly cracked his skull

That's horrible

You need to get a weapon

Are you kidding?

It's Colorado

There's like a school shooting every week

We have see-through backpacks and metal detectors

I'd go to actual jail

Yeah

That sucks

Wish you were here

Me too

I never thought I'd miss Jefferson High

I guess things can always get worse

That's the spirit

But they'll get better

They have to

There are some kids who hang out in the graveyard down the street from the school and smoke cigarettes

Maybe I should start smoking

You would die

If you tried to smoke a cigarette

Instantly

Probably not good for your clarinet career either

Dad smoked

Never in front of us

He'd go out to the yard

Right at the edge where it met the woods

And have a cigarette watching the sunset

He let me try one once

I think to discourage me

It felt like I was breathing glass

I almost cried

I miss him

Yeah

That gives me an idea though

I made the compass

I took a little magnet out of the clasp on my bracelet

And glued it right over the N on the disk

But I still don't know where to put it

I tried the burners on the stove

But the direction points right into the wall

And the metal on the stove keeps messing with the magnet

I don't think dad would have been so clumsy with it

I even tried the burn mark on the linoleum

From when Bean was cooking hot dogs and then just put the pot on the floor

But that wasn't the right size

Now I'm thinking it's not the kitchen

Smoke

Fire

Hell

It was dad's smoking spot

Brb

13

OCTOBER 3

Sorry! Sorry!

Mom caught me sneaking out and hid my phone again

She's really losing it

Bean is on a rampage

He broke the toaster

Like that will bring dad back

No more Eggos I guess

What are we going to eat for breakfast?

Or lunch

Or dinner

Lol

That's the only thing mom knows how to cook

But that was a mistake on my part

I got too excited

I should have waited until morning

Not gone out at 11pm

How are you?

Fine

Great!

:/

Not fine?

The same I guess

I guess that's a win

Want to talk about it?

No

There's nothing to talk about

14

OCTOBER 4

You won't believe it

What?

I found it

The place for the compass

Uh huh

Really

I went to dad's smoking spot and it was so obvious

The bird bath

It has a little notch in the middle

And it was full of water from the rain

I slipped the disk onto the notch and it floated on the water

The magnet slid north

And the notch pointed right into the woods

And when I looked closely I saw there was an old deer path there

So the only question is

Am I supposed to follow the path

Or go straight

And for how long?

Maybe I'll try walking 666 yards

Keeping with the devil theme

I have a question

How does your dad know how to do all this

Design these elaborate puzzles?

That involve codes and compasses and magnets

Dad was really smart

If he'd finished high school he would have gone to college and been an engineer or a doctor or anything

But mom got pregnant with me

Just because he wasn't educated didn't mean he wasn't smart

I'm not saying your dad wasn't smart

I'm just saying

What?

I'm saying you're smart too!

Really smart

And maybe you're so smart you're finding clues that maybe your dad didn't leave

Maybe this is your puzzle

Not his

Oh I see

I'm wracked with grief

And in order to avoid the pain I'm feeling

My genius brain makes up a fun fantasy mystery

No

I don't know

I mean

I'm worried about you

It was fine before

But I don't want you wandering into the woods

You know?

That's another level

It's dangerous

What if you get lost?

I know how to walk in the woods

Dad and I would go hiking all the time

I just don't want you wandering around the woods looking for something that might not be there

Might not?

I know that

Dad's dead okay

How many times are you going to make me write it?

Dead dead dead

He might have died before he finished the game

Or

There's something he really really really wanted me to find

And I'm going to find it

...

!

Hey, since we're psychoanalyzing, let me try

Your life sucks

You hate your life

You have no friends

Your dad's alive

But he thinks you're a loser

And you see me

The one person you could pity

Get super excited about something

And you want to take it away

That was really mean

I'm not trying to take anything away from you

Go do your puzzle

I hope you do find something

CIA files

A copy of the declaration of independence

Gold bars

The holy grail

Hello?

You're just going to ignore me?

Whatever

15
OCTOBER 5

Hey

I'm sorry

I'm sorry

Rori

I'm sorry

OCTOBER 6

I know you're mad at me but please

Just let me know if you're ok

17

OCTOBER 7

RUOK?

OCTOBER 8

Hi

Sorry

I

I'm in a bad way

But I'm okay

I'm sorry I said those things

I didn't mean it

You were right anyway

I

Found something

But

I don't think dad wanted me to find it

Wait

You found something?

What did you find?

I followed the deer path

It went pretty far

A mile and a half at least

Uphill mostly

I left Saturday morning

I brought snacks and water

And a rain jacket and a flashlight

Just in case

And a whistle

And my phone of course

But I lost reception immediately

Those stupid hills

Every once and a while I found a cigarette butt

So I knew I was on the right track

But

Dad always picked up his butts so

That was weird

And the path was pretty clear

So he must have used it pretty frequently

It wound up the hill

At one point it cut through an old chain link fence

I don't think it was on our property

State forest maybe

After about an hour I saw something

What?!

It was a hut

Or a shack

Small

Made of old wood

And falling apart

It had a window but the glass was broken

I got really scared that someone was there

I called out but no one answered

Then I threw a rock at the door

In case there was a bear or something

That's so creepy

I was pretty creeped out

There was junk everywhere

An old car

And a toilet

Rusty pipes

But the woods were really thick

So I don't know where it could have come from

There were old car seats around a fire pit

Don't tell me the pit was still smoking

No

It was cold and wet

There was glass everywhere

Beer bottles

And liquor bottles

I was freaked out

I almost went home but

I felt something

It's weird

Don't get mad but I felt like

I could hear something

Like my dad was calling my name

...

I know!

Maybe it was in my head

But just listen

I went to the door and

Pushed it open

And the inside was gross

There were posters of naked women all over the walls and ceiling

And there were bullet holes in the walls

The sun shone through in dusty little beams

Omg

Yeah

More booze

An old office chair

And some wet magazines

I think the roof leaked

It smelled awful

I would have run right away as fast as I could

I wanted to

But I thought...

I don't know what I was thinking

There was an old radio

Battery operated

It was still hissing static

So maybe that's what I thought I heard

Makes sense

I wanted to get out of there

But I searched the place and found

Something under the desk

It was a box

An old metal toolbox

It was dad's

I'd seen him carry it into the basement sometimes

So I took it

It was heavy

I wanted to see what was inside but

That place was freaking me out so

I carried it home

Well not all the way home

I stopped about a quarter mile from home

By a brook

There was a big oak there with a

Hole in its trunk

So I could hide it there

Mom's always searching my room

Then I opened it

What was inside?

...

A gun

What?

A revolver

It was loaded

And there were some loose bullets too

Sometimes at night

When I was in bed

I'd hear gunshots in the distance

I wonder if that was dad

Holy...

What are you going to do?

Keep it

It was dad's so now it's mine

Don't worry

I'm not going to shoot mom

Dad never taught me to shoot

I'll sell it for my

Bugout fund

Oh...

There's more

In the toolbox

A bottle of white pills

No label

Looks like he took them from another bottle

Weird

Maybe they're painkillers

Dad hurt his back working construction

That's why he had to quit and get a job as a security guard

Or they were sleep meds

He could never fall asleep

Maybe I'll slip one to mom and see what happens

Not funny

It's a little funny

I'll mail them to you and you can give them to the D&D club

Ha ha

Was that it?

No

A pack of cigarettes

Some shooters of rum

A card I made him

That's nice

Yep

Kept it right next to his cigs and rum

I'm honored

I didn't know dad drank so much

Maybe it wasn't that much

Or just a once and a while thing

Sure

Maybe

There was something else

What?

A spiral notebook

His diary

I didn't know dad kept a diary

Oh

You're not going to read it

Are you?

Well

Why not?

I'm asking

It's an invasion of privacy

True

And people write things in their diaries they need to express but don't want to say to other people

Yes

And you could read something you can't unread

Like what?

I don't know

But you said yourself he didn't want you to find it

It looks like he was trying pretty hard to hide some parts of his life from you

Yeah

I know

But I can't help thinking

What if

What if I am supposed to read it

Maybe he did want me to find it

He wanted it so bad he didn't care what I saw

Go ahead

Tell me I'm stupid

No

I get it

I dunno

Maybe you'll learn more about him

Oh crap

Mom's calling

Literally

Out in the yard screaming my name

No wonder dad was hiding in a shack

G2G

19

OCTOBER 9

I know it's late

I can't sleep

I just keep thinking about the diary

I thought I heard dad's voice

Like he was in the woods

By the brook

Calling to me

It must have been a dream

I have to read it

20

OCTOBER 10

I did it

I snuck out right at dawn

And got the diary

I opened it

The first entry is from just a year ago

Right around the time he started working for Stillwater

Dad's handwriting is really bad

It's like hieroglyphics

I have to decipher it

And it got wet at some point

So it's kind of moldy

But...

It's pretty rough

And there are drawings

Scribbles of

I don't know

Faces?

Horrible faces if they're faces

He just scrawls them in out of nowhere

I don't think it's us

Me and mom and Bean

I hope not

I know dad wasn't living his best life but

I didn't realize he was so unhappy and

I dunno

Disturbed

It's really dark

Do you think

Do you think maybe he wanted to die?

21

OCTOBER 11

Hey

No!

No no no

It was an accident

And not his fault

A truck swerved out of its lane

And hit him

Don't do this to yourself

Get rid of it

Burn it

Have a ceremony

Say goodbye

Let him rest

Don't go inventing stories

You're just torturing yourself

Your brain is trying to make sense of something senseless

But you don't have to

Yeah

Thanks

You're right

I should just burn it all

But the gun

And the pills

I just can't stop thinking

Everyone in Jefferson has a gun

And your dad was in chronic pain

You said yourself

There are a bunch of reasons for him to have those pills

Yeah

I don't know what I expected

Not rainbows and stickers and poetry definitely

But

Not this

Half of it doesn't make any sense

It's just long run-on sentences

And then the drawings

And then at the bottom of the page he'll scrawl something like

I CAN HEAR YOU

In all caps

Practically carved in with the pen

What?

Maybe it's part of the game?

Or a puzzle he was working on

Maybe

Dad never tried to scare the crap out of me in any of his games

Here

[Upload failed]

Ugh these stupid mountains

I'll send it to you when I have wifi in school

22

OCTOBER 12

[Journal1.jpeg]

What do you think?

What...

What is that?

One of dad's drawings

Looks like a bunch of faces in the trees to me

...

Maybe

"3:31 a.m. Heard another voice. Saw face reflected in the window glass. It was there. I know it was there. Almost first light. Hopefully the voice will stop. When I close my eyes I see the face again. He's dead. I know he's dead. They're all dead."

This is from the diary?

Yeah

One of the entries

There are pages and pages and pages like this

"Midnight. Screams. I ran to the lobby but no one was there. No one has been here for years. The screams don't stop. They follow me back to the booth. Now they follow me home."

And

"They're begging me now. I can hear them. They're out in the parking lot. They want me to come in. I can't see them but they're there. Control says one more false alarm and I'm canned. They can't hear the screams! Stop! Shut up! Shut up! Shut up!"

...

I think your dad had PTSD maybe

Or he was high as balls

Or crazy

But this is from work

All of his night shifts

Maybe he was bored

And trying to make it more exciting

Maybe it's a screenplay he was working on

Does this read like a screenplay??

Anyway

That happened

At least once

The false alarm

Mom was chewing dad out because he called the cops up there

Because he thought he heard someone screaming in the building

They did a whole manhunt and he got an official demerit

So he was definitely afraid of getting fired

But

If that happened

Maybe these other things did too

"I saw her again. She was grinning at me from the windows of the lobby. Her face was too long. She wanted me to come. I took out the gun but when I looked away to load it she was gone. I couldn't close my eyes after that. I took another caffeine pill so I'd be ready. She'll be back."

That explains the gun and the pills

I guess the pills could be caffeine

But maybe they're something else

He must have felt pretty threatened to buy a gun

You think someone was messing with him?

It's a strong possibility

Bored kids

Or meth heads

Tweakers

Or squatters

There's enough of those in Jefferson

Look at this

"11:03. It's starting early. A howl. I pray it's an animal. Then I hear that laugh. Someone sniggering. I can feel them right outside the booth. They're ducking down. So close. I could lean out the window and see them staring up at me. I'm afraid to see their face. Those eyes. That grin. They're right there. I can hear them. Stop laughing at me!"

Whoa

How much of this did you type up?

I'm typing all of it as I go

In study hall

To look for clues

I thought you didn't think this was actually a puzzle game

That's what I thought at first

But

This isn't a diary

It's a record

Maybe dad wanted someone to read it

23

OCTOBER 13

I just had a horrible thought

But I have to know

You aren't messing with me, right?

I'm getting messed with all day

The drawing club

D&D club

And now people think it's funny to mess with me

Like they'll act friendly and then ghost me

Or like steal my backpack and tie it to the flagpole

Every time it happens it's funnier to them

That I'm so gullible to think someone could like me

And last night I had this horrible thought that maybe it is me

That I'm not just the new kid

That there's something wrong with me

So I'll always get picked on and messed with

So please

Please tell me you aren't messing with me

Pretty messed up of you to ask

No I'm not messing with you

I'd have to be some kind of crazy genius

Or an entire D&D club all working together

Kidding

This is real

I wish it weren't

But it is

And listen

You're not going to get messed with forever

Someone else will transfer in

People will get bored and forget you

You'll find your people

Ok

Thanks

I really hate it here

24

OCTOBER 14

More crazy stuff

"They were all there last night. All the voices and faces. They were behind the glass in the lobby. I could see them, crowded in, all laughing and crying and screaming. I put in ear plugs but I could still hear them. I closed my eyes and when I opened them they were right there pressed against the glass of the booth."

What does he mean

They were in the lobby?

He worked as the night watchman for the abandoned Stillwater facility

I tried to find information on it but there's nothing

Not about what they were doing or when it was built

Just an article about it closing down

And the jobs being lost

Stillwater is a military contractor

So they could have been doing all kinds of shady things

But it had been abandoned for a while when dad got the job

I actually went with mom a few times to drop dad off after his Buick died

The facility is in a valley

You go through a chain link gate and then there's a long, private road

It's kind of falling apart

The facility is really big and ugly

Like a big gray box

The parking lot is big too

There must have been a lot of people there once

Dad's booth was like a crappy little temporary structure

Right in the middle of the parking lot

Kind of like a toll booth

It had windows all around it

The lobby he's talking about is the lobby of the building

But the doors were locked and chained shut when I was there

So I don't know how people could get in

Dad was excited for the job at first

He was just happy to get a job where he could sit down

But I remember even then thinking how creepy it was

We dropped him off at sundown

His shift was 9 to 6

The building was so dark

There were just of couple of dim yellow lights around his booth

The place looked haunted for sure

So creepy

You think he was seeing ghosts?

Dad didn't believe in ghosts

I don't know what I think

Maybe the company left a bunch of chemicals there

And they were leaking out

Making dad see things

Maybe that's why they came and took all his stuff

And he hid this for me to find

But why

What did he want you to do with it?

Maybe he just wanted me to know

Obviously he couldn't tell mom

She'd just freak

And accuse him of trying to quit again

Like he didn't almost break his back at his last job

And he just chose to quit

Or maybe there's evidence here

Of liability

And he wants me to get a lawyer

And we sue the company

Like Erin Brockovich

I need to finish the diary

25

OCTOBER 15

<

You won't believe this

Oh boy

"That sound was back. It sounds like a creaking door that keeps opening and opening. It's out there in the lot. I can see them moving just outside the edge of the yellow lights. It's coming through my phone. The radio. The creaking. They're coming closer. I can feel it. Whenever I look away it runs towards me in the darkness."

Oh man

This is freaking me out

Me too

Dad drew something too

I think it's the lights

Or whatever is outside the lights

They look like feet or hands

And at the bottom of the page

He wrote a name

Will Richardson

And circled it a million times

I think I know him

Wasn't that our geography teacher in 6th grade?

No

Different Will Richardson

I looked him up

I even used mom's credit card to pay for one of those online people searches

He was the guy who had dad's job before him

What?!

Yeah

And he's dead

No

Yep

Died in a boating accident

Then dad took his job

"Boating accident"?

Right?

Could that be any more suspicious?

He went out on his little fishing dingy and never came back

Body floated to shore a few days later

There's an article about it in the Jefferson Sun

He was drinking and abusing oxycontin

A bunch of police reports too

All in the months before he died

Before that he was squeaky clean

Then suddenly

DUIs

Disorderly conduct

Drunk in public

I wish I could talk to his widow

That's a terrible idea

Don't worry

She moved

Sold the house

A family lives there now

Three really blond kids

And a black lab running around the yard

You went there?!

I had to

You have to admit

This is all suspicious as heck

Dad thought so

He looked the guy up

I agree

It's a really weird coincidence

I dunno though

The woods always creeped me out at night

There's woods here too

But not the same

There was something about Jefferson that made them extra creepy

I can't imagine being stuck in a little tin can

Night after night

Next to that big creepy building

All alone

It would get to me

My imagination would run wild

Doesn't mean there's any toxic chemicals involved

Or evil conspiracies

He was taking caffeine pills

And he was basically doing most of the housework too

And taking care of you and Bean

He probably wasn't sleeping well

All that combined

It's a lot

Yeah

Yeah you're right

26

OCTOBER 16

"Now I see them everywhere. They follow me home. I see their faces in the reflection in the windows. They're in the mirror. They're in the glass. In the shadows at the edge of the lights. They won't leave me alone."

He's talking about our house!

You think the people he was seeing followed him home?

That's so scary

They know where you live

You have to call the cops

Yeah right

And tell them what?

My dad's crazy diary said he saw scary people in the house?

Anyway, it's not like I

Or Bean or mom saw anything

Mom would have ultra mega freaked if weirdos had showed up

At least start locking the door

Or something

Get a security camera

One of those video recording doorbells

Not a bad idea

I don't know how I'd convince mom though

Or where we'd get the money

I'm worried about you

I think we're fine

It's not like we have anything to steal

And I have a gun now

That does not make me less worried

27

OCTOBER 17

Read this

"I heard them calling to me last night. I got up and looked out the window. They were there in the trees. White bodies. White faces. Pale twisted slivers. They called for me to come. Gracie didn't hear them. Sprout and Bean didn't hear them. No one can hear them but me. I almost woke Gracie. But I knew she couldn't see. They hadn't come for her."

That doesn't sound like tweakers

It sounds like a cult

It sounds like he was hallucinating

There are pages of this

Seeing faces out of the corner of his eye

Hearing noises

Feeling like he's being watched

And before you ask

No

Dad did not have a history of mental illness

Other than depression

But that's literally everyone

It does sound like he had some kind of psychotic break though

Maybe it's like what you said

The long nights

The pills

The pressure to take care of us

Got to him

And he cracked

I'm sorry

This is a lot

How are you holding up?

I'm okay

But

This is weird

...

I don't want to tell you

??

Please just don't make fun of me

It's vulnerable

I feel like

I feel like he's talking to me sometimes

That makes sense

You're reading his diary

No

I mean literally

I can hear him

It's so faint

But sometimes

If it's quiet at night

I can hear his voice

You're tired

Make sure you're

Getting enough rest

Take care of yourself

Maybe take a break from the diary

I will

I'm almost done the diary anyway

How are you doing?

Pretty good, actually!

That's great!

Yeah

Someone else who tried to join D&D club also got kicked out

They dropped a mentos in his coke and it sprayed everywhere

Said he got hit by a fireball and died

But he was way cooler than me

He poured the rest of his coke over the DM

And told them all off with a bunch of swear words

Then he sat with me at lunch and asked if I wanted to play Magic the Gathering with him

Awesome!

It's happening

I'm trying not to get my hopes up

But he's really cool

He's on the autism spectrum

You wouldn't really notice

But he just says whatever he thinks

And he doesn't lie so

I'm excited!

I can't wait to hear all about your new friendship!

28

OCTOBER 19

"It's happening to me. I can feel myself detaching. I'm so much lighter now. They're all there waiting for me. They need my help. I have to go free them."

"I can't open the chain to the lobby. I don't have a key. Someone was inside watching me. I saw their shadow. They hid from my light."

"There's another way in. It's around the back. I can hear them calling. Their shadows watch me from the trees. I can hear them calling from the pipe. I'm going in."

What the heck!?

He broke in

What if he was right?

What if people were watching him?

I thought maybe he was hallucinating

Because of the chemicals they left behind

But what if

What if they didn't leave the chemicals behind

What if they gave them to him on purpose

What if the facility is still open

And they were experimenting on him

Just like they experimented on the guy before him?

Hello?

29

OCTOBER 20

"I found the pipe. It's an exhaust vent for a furnace. The top was twisted off; maybe it came down in the storms. It left a jagged opening. I crawled inside. It smelled of rust and mold. I crawled until I came to a rusted grate. I pushed it aside with my bare hands. It crumbled and cut me."

"My blood mixed with the slime and the mold. I crawled and crawled and then the pipe opened into the room."

"It was a morgue. A crematorium. I saw the char. The furnace. The slots in the wall for the bodies. I saw the bodies lying in their beds. Black shadows. They watched me as I left. They're always watching me from the shadows."

Uh he came home one night filthy

With cuts all over his hands

Wouldn't talk about it

Went right to bed

Was this what he was doing??

"I saw them in the halls. White faces flickering in the glass. The voices were louder now. They were screaming. They were burning! They were hurting! They knew I was there. They're watching me."

"I was too late. I found them. Ash. They're all ash now from the furnaces. Burned away. I can still hear their screams. They died and came back. They died and came back. They died and came back. And they couldn't stop coming back even burned to ash."

He found bodies!

They were burning people in there

Experimenting on them

Hello!?

Could you say something?

30

OCTOBER 21

"They won't leave me alone. They won't leave the house. They're in the shadows. I see them in the glass. I see them in the mirror. They're screaming. Laughing. They want me to go back. They want something. Shut up. Shut up! SHUT UP! What do you want?"

"I saw one sitting next to Sprout. She was eating cereal. It was sitting right next to her. Laughing. It was so pale. Its eyes were black. It was Will. It was Will. He was laughing at me. Sprout couldn't see him, but he was there."

Omg

I remember that

Dad was drinking his coffee

His eyes were so red and wild

He was looking at me funny

Past me

Like he wasn't even seeing me

It was two days before he died

"They died and came back. They died and came back. They died and came back. Even burned to ash."

"They won't leave me alone. I have to go back."

Anything?

No?

31

OCTOBER 23

"I crawled back through the pipe. The bodies had moved since I was there. They watched me from the shadows. I heard their screams echo from the cold ash. I put it in my pocket. Is that what they wanted?"

"I found the room. All the hospital beds in rows. This is where they died. Over and over. The shelves were empty. No medicines. No drugs. No machines. No computers. What brought them back? Why can't they leave? They watched me from the glass."

"I heard a crash and ran. My heart burst as I ran. I heard their screams and laughs. I slipped and fell and crawled under a desk. I hid and hid. It was quiet. The ash on my hands mixed with the tears on my face. I heard footsteps and ran. They're after me."

"I found myself in the morgue. I heard the creak of the footsteps. I crawled into the furnace and hid myself in the ash. The bodies watched from the shadows. I know what they want. They want me to stay with them."

That was from the night he died

He broke in

And then wrote that

And then a truck runs him off the road

I went with mom to ID the body

He had ash on him

His hands

His clothes

His face...

Not much to see there

It barely even registered

But now

Oh man

I don't even know what to think

32

OCTOBER 25

Okay I checked

No shootings

Floods

Fires

Or hurricanes in Colorado

So I'll assume you've been kidnapped

By space pirates

As I see it here are the possibilities

1. Dad dies in an accident

2. Dad suffers contamination left by evil corporation and dies in accident caused by rapidly deteriorating health

3. Same as above but dad is deliberately experimented on

4. Dad breaks in, finds dangerous secrets, and is killed by evil corporation, in which case I am also in danger. Puzzle game was a way of getting the diary to me and I should send it to a journalist

5. Ghosts haunt and kill dad

Just spitballing

But

He keeps saying they died and came back

It's written all over the diary

What if Stillwater was doing an experiment to try and bring people back from the dead?

And it worked

But they didn't come back as living bodies

But something else?

No

That sounds crazy

But

What else could that mean?

Ideas???

33

OCTOBER 27

So what?

You're just going to ghost me?

Not even talk to me anymore?

Did you get turned to stone again?

I'm going crazy over here

34

OCTOBER 28

Hi

Finally!!!

We need to talk

Oh boy

I've been talking to Trevor

Who is Trevor???

My friend I play MTG with

And he says you are clearly messing with me

What?

Come on, Rori

You're talking about dead bodies and ghosts

You expect me to believe that?

I expect you to be my friend

Wtf does Trevor know?

I'm not sure I believe it

But my dad wrote it

And I believe my dad

I need you to help me make sense of it

Yeah

That's the point

You're trying to make sense

Of something senseless

And inventing this whole conspiracy

To try and regain control

And I played along because I thought it was what you needed

And I didn't want you to

I didn't want you to hurt yourself again

But it's gotten to the point where it's not healthy

Not for me

And not for you

So please

Stop

You "played along"?!?

You thought I'd slit my wrists if you didn't humor me?

I cut once! When I was really really really low

WTF

And here I thought you were such a good friend

But actually *you* were just messing with *me*

I do want to be your friend!

I am your friend

I just can't do this anymore

oh James

Or dear dear

Dear dear dear dear

James

I wish to GOD I was making this up

You think I don't want closure?

Some normal cry till I puke grief

And then peace?

Knowing my dad is up in heaven

With the angels

Beaming down at me

I wish it to God

Because

That's not what I think

I think he's still here

Trapped

On Earth

Suffering

I haven't even told you half the things
I've seen

Because I know you'll be skeptical

You won't believe me

I can hear you rolling your eyes at me with
every text

But I hear him too

He's moving around the living room in the
middle of the night

He's calling my name

I wake up and see him standing in the
doorway in the dark

Or leaning over me for a goodnight kiss

For a second

Then he's gone

I can see him standing at his smoke spot in
the twilight

He watches me from the woods at night

He's in the mirror

In the glass

Even though we cremated him

We burned him to ash

His ash sits on the mantle

And he's still here

I don't give a damn if you believe me

But I thought you cared

...

I do care

I'm worried about you

But I can't play this game anymore

Please

Seek help

I hope Trevor pushes you off a cliff

Don't text me from the hospital

35

OCTOBER 30

I don't expect you to answer this

In fact I hope you don't

You pig

But I'm texting you so there will be a record

Guess what?!

Puzzle game is on

Dad numbered some of his entries

Totally out of order

And what does it mean?

Why, just write them all down in order

And put a slash in the middle

What do you get?

Latitude and longitude

GPS coordinates

They head right to the pipe dad talked about

How do I know?

I'm there now

[Upload failed]

[Upload failed]

Whatever it's a picture of the pipe

Didn't even have to steal the car

Mom thinks I'm at the library studying for the SATs

As you can see

It's noon here

So no ghosts yet

I'm so dumb that I believe in them and they scare me a lot

Tell Trevor I said hi

He's so smart and cool

How did dad fit in here?

I can barely make it

Oh it's a lot wider now

Gross though

And there's the grate

Yep open

Ow it's sharp

Gotta be careful cuz I'm really dumb

Okay I'm through

Whew

Not fun

Still no ghosts

Oh what the heck

It curves down

Dad was right

It's an exhaust vent or something

Ugh it smells

How far do I have to go

Aha!

Here's the hole

I guess dad was tall enough to lower himself down

I'll have to drop

Okay I think I see the bottom

Okay

Yolo

Wait

I chickened out

For real this time

Here I go

36

OCTOBER 31

Ow

Oh god

I fell

The edge was so slippery

I can't get back up

I must have hit my head and passed out

It's already midnight

Okay

I think I might be concussed

My head is killing me

I have a lump the size of a grapefruit on my forehead

Smashed my headlamp

It's so dark in here

And cold

Where am I?

I need to rest

I'm just going to take a little nap

I hear something

Footsteps

I don't know if I should call out or not

Mom's gotta be freaking out

I gotta get out of here

I can't get back up

I'm scared

I crawled forward

And found a hatch

It's part of a big boiler or something

It smells like oil

The footsteps are gone

I can hear something else

Someone's talking

Someone's here

Dad?

I crawled out

I'm in the morgue

Just like dad wrote about

Some of the drawers are open

No bodies

Thank god

I hear something

Something's moving

My calls aren't going through

I don't even know if you're getting these

But if you are

Help me

No one is responding

I'm alone

No one can hear me

The furnace is full of ash

I looked

It's just like dad said

It's a crematorium

They were burning the bodies

I'm using the light from my phone

I'm running out of batteries

I'm going to try and get to the front door

I saw someone!

They walked across the hallway

Just a shadow

I don't think they saw me

If you see these get help

Call 911

The police

Firemen

Anything

I don't care

I have to get out of here

Someone is screaming

I can hear it echoing down the hall

I'm trying to get away from it

I think I saw a face in the glass

I'm hiding

I'm in a cleaning closet

I think they saw me

Something is moving around in the next room

I'm sorry I wasn't a better friend

I'm sorry Bean

I'm sorry mom

I'm sorry dad

I'm sorry

I'm sorry

I ran

They kept getting closer and closer

I ran and came to the stairs

They only went down

Down down

Down

Someone was laughing

It's so dark down here

I can only see with my phone

But then

They'll see me

It's quiet

Thank god

Dad?

It's dad

I can hear him

He's trying to help me

I'll follow his voice

He's calling me

It's definitely dad

I can almost make out what he's saying

It's close now

There's ash on the floor

It's okay

Dad's here now

I can see him

He's at the end of the hall

He wants to show me something

He's smiling

He came back for me

No!

He hurt me

It wasn't dad

It couldn't be dad

Dad wouldn't hurt me

I ran

They're everywhere

I can see them in the glass

Dad!

He's screaming too

I have to get out of here

I

37

NOVEMBER 1

Rori !???

MISSED CALL
MISSED CALL
MISSED CALL
MISSED CALL

!????!

RORI!!!

RUOK?!

ABOUT THE AUTHOR

Andy Futuro is a time traveler from the future. He lives in a tent and is often lost.

To learn more, visit:

andyfuturo.com

To subscribe to updates, visit:

andyfuturo.substack.com

ALSO BY ANDY FUTURO

The Special Sin Series

No Dogs in Philly

Cloud Country

Dirtbag Lit

Josephine Wins Again

Music Available On

Spotify

Bandcamp

Apple Music

YouTube Music

And more...

Printed in Great Britain
by Amazon

51308048R00083